Arctic Butterfly

by

NANCY GARFIELD WOODBRIDGE

ILLUSTRATIONS BY
MARVIN PARACUELLES

To order additional copies of this book, contact:
Xlibris
1-888-795-4274
www.Xlibris.com
Orders@Xlibris.com

DEDICATION

This book is dedicated to my husband, George Woodbridge, my sons, Maurice and Josh, and to Katie and Sarah, to Stephanie B. and CC, to Mike G. and to my father, Sol, a most wise and caring artist.

Beams of light are reflected across the bright, white snow as Kula watches her grandfather shout at the Arctic dogs who are pulling their sled across the tundra. Kula looks up at the dark, wintry sky, and sees that it is heavily streaked with silver clouds. The sun beats down on tiny hillocks of powdered, white snow as Kula thinks about the frozen lake they have just crossed. She sees that it is twilight and knows that the darkness of night will soon come to the Arctic.

"Hurry home," shouts Kula's grandfather Ahloo as he whips the dogs faster to move them along. "We want to go home to our village," he shouts loudly as frost clings to the breath of his words.

2

As Kula looks across at the wintry sky in the distance, far, far down the hill she can see the smoke rising from the igloos. "We are home, we are home, grandfather," shouts Kula. Several minutes later, their sled comes to a sudden stop.

Kula jumps up and runs towards her own igloo. She embraces her mother, Elisia, who is waiting for them near the entrance. They enter the igloo and inside a blue-orange light flickers against a wall of ice. Kula steps onto a sealskin blanket. Her mother smiles and says, "Welcome home." Kula takes off her little jacket, *kiviak*, and hangs it up to dry.

Now, Grandfather Ahloo enters the igloo, and he says with a smile, "We have brought wonderful things to you from afar; come and open these sacks and see --"

Kula's mother opens the sacks and shouts, "Matches, sugar and tea." She is smiling. Her face glows in the blue-orange light of the soapstone lamp, and inside her *kiviak* hood lies Kamoona, Kula's baby sister. Kamoona is asleep.

In a corner of the igloo lies a small puppy who is all curled up in a ball. He looks like a round, fur cap lying on the floor. Kula runs over to him. "Wake up, Chimo, I am home . . . It is I, Kula, here."

The little pup looks up sleepily, and seeing Kula, he jumps up and races around and around her feet in small circles. His tail is wagging furiously with excitement.

Kula's father, Pauli, enters the igloo.

"Welcome back, Kula and Ahloo," he says, embracing them.

Kula is very, very tired from her long trip to the trading post and lies down on her sealskin blanket and falls asleep. Outside, the wind blows great piles of snow in all directions. The dark, blue, Arctic night has come, and the stars glitter like snowflakes above the land. A round, silvery moon rises in the deep, blue sky. Now, Kula's mother and father and grandfather and baby sister are all asleep beneath their sealskin blankets. The dogs are asleep, too. It is gently quiet in the Arctic night as only the breath of the wind can be heard.

In the morning, Pauli, Kula's father, prepares to leave on a hunting trip. He will catch seal and polar bear and will fish beneath the frozen lake. Kula wants to go with him, but her father says, "No, Kula, you are a little girl . . . and you cannot hunt with the men . . . you must stay home with the others now."

Pauli readies the sleds and leaves on his trip. The family waves "good bye" to him and wishes him "good luck." Kula watches her father leave. She is standing outside as she sees him disappear into the distance, and she is very unhappy.

Grandfather Ahloo says, "What is wrong? Tell me, little one."

"I want to go hunting with my father," says Kula, "but he says I am a girl and I cannot go with him."

Ahloo is standing outside the igloo and his old eyes gaze out across the treeless country as he looks into the distance at miles of tundra spreading out. As Ahloo stares at the gigantic mountains of ice and snow glistening like jeweled palaces in the sunlight, he says, "Be patient, Kula. One day your time will come, and you will be a mother. Hunting is for men." Kula is silent, but very, very upset. She cannot understand why girls are barred from hunting. "I am strong," she thinks, "and I can learn how to hunt . . . but they won't let me."

Suddenly, the sounds of great flocks of geese are heard as they fly overhead and they both look up at the sky. Kula whispers to Ahloo, "I am worried about my father . . . the flocks of geese are a bad sign for hunters."

"Do not fear, Kula, the Goddess Sedna will protect your father."

"If the Goddess Sedna protects my father when he hunts, why can't she protect me?" asks Kula.

"I have said before, you will do more than hunt when you are a grown woman."

Kula was not satisfied, but said nothing.

For six days and six nights, Pauli does not return from his hunting trip. Elisia is very worried about him, and Kula, too, is fearful that her father will not come back home. She thinks of the dangers of the north. On this night, Kula dreams that her father's eyes are frozen shut by the snow, and that he cannot find his way back to the igloo. She wakes up in the dark igloo and is shivering with fear. Perhaps, Pauli has fallen into the open sea or floated away on a piece of ice, never to return again.

Kula cannot sleep. Just before morning, she dresses quickly and goes outside. She carries her little pup Chimo with her. The others are asleep.

When her mother, Elisia wakes up, she doesn't see Kula inside the igloo. Elisia calls, "Kula, Kula, where are you?" Kula does not answer.

Kula and Chimo are gone. Elisia begins to cry. Grandfather Ahloo tries to comfort her. "Do not worry, Elisia, they will

both return," he says very gently. But Elisia cannot believe him. She is weak with sorrow and fear for her loved ones.

By morning, Kula has wandered far away. She is searching for her father, and she cannot find him. She sits down in the snow and weeps for him, and for herself because she is lost. Kula has wandered many miles from her igloo.

Elisia and Grandfather Ahloo tell the people of the village that Pauli and Kula are both lost. The people of the village are shocked. The men of the village ready their sleds to travel across the snow in search of them. They do not know if they will find them.

Many miles away, Kula is walking around and around in a small circle. The white snow is spinning around her head. She feels dizzy as she looks across at the deserted land.

"The seal Goddess Sedna is laughing at me," says Kula, "she has brought me bad luck, not good luck."

A tear falls from her eye. It turns to silver as the cold air hits the tear and sparkles on Kula's cheek holding the golden rays of the sun inside it. It forms a rainbow of light against her dark skin. Deep inside Kula there is pain and fear.

"I am lost," she whispers, "and . . . I cannot find my father."

Kula is terrified. She wanders and wanders about in the snow drifts. Chimo, the little puppy, scampers behind her. Kula looks around her at the vast stretches of white snow. Far, far as her eye can see, she searches for a sign of her father, but she sees only snowflakes dancing in the cold wind.

Kula is shivering and trembling with fear as she wanders around and around. The sun is a blinding, golden circle. The snow is blazing white. The ice has turned to silver, as Kula gazes out over the land. Looking far beyond into the distance, she sees only more snow.

"I am alone," she says. "I will surely die because I am lost, and now, no one can find me . . ."

Now Kula bends down in the snow. She is weeping. Her eyelids flutter gently for a moment as she brushes away her tears. A gigantic Arctic butterfly flies around Kula's head and she reaches out her hand to touch it. But the butterfly floats away in the icy, blue sky. Its silvery, white wings look like lace as their patterns flicker and flutter against the wind. For a moment, the butterfly floats back and perches on her little, brown finger. Kula tries to hold the butterfly, but it flies swiftly away into the distance, and soon becomes just a speck over the barren, white land.

"Chimo, we are doomed," says Kula, as she sits down in the soft, white snow. Chimo darts around and around, jumping up and down. "What is it, Chimo, what is it?" Kula asks.

And now in the distance, they hear a loud, crackling noise. Kula puts her hand over her eyes. "I am afraid, Chimo, for I can see nothing coming. I can only hear a terrible, loud noise."

Suddenly there is a great shout. Chimo jumps up into the air. "Kula, Kula." She looks up and sees her father running towards her. He lifts her up and holds her tightly in his arms.

16

"What are you doing out here?" asks Pauli. He is stunned to find Kula so far away from the igloo.

"I am lost," says Kula, but she does not wish to tell her father why.

"It is good that I found you, child," says Pauli who now places her on his own sled and moves up to the front of it himself. "You must really want to go hunting with me," he says as he whips the dogs now. "Even though you are a girl, perhaps, next time I go . . . you will come along with me," he continues.

Kula smiles now, for that is what she wanted. As she rides back home on her father's sled and breathes a sigh of relief, she closes her eyes and leans back to rest. She listens as her father sings an ancient hunting song:

"Giant snow hills cannot conceal my seal.

Sedna, the laughing spirit rises from the sea

And greets me with her magic.

But giant, icy waters will not conceal

My seal."

Kula is happy now because her father has finally understood her feelings. His sled is loaded with two seals and one polar bear. The hunting was so good that he was delayed for several days in order to catch as much as possible. Flocks of grey geese honk in the sky as Chimo curls up in Kula's lap. Now the sky turns green and pink and blue and yellow with strange, Arctic lights as they arrive at their village.

There is much shouting and noise when they pull up. Elisia hugs and kisses her husband and her daughter. Grandfather Ahloo stands quietly by as he watches Kula getting off her father's sled.

"Kula, you found your father after all," says Ahloo. "No, Grandfather, I was . . . lost. I didn't find him . . . he found ME. The only thing I found was a beautiful, Arctic butterfly with silvery, lacey white wings but . . . it just flew away very quickly and left me . . . all . . . alone. It is so good to be home," Kula whispers to Grandfather Ahloo. "And my father, Pauli has promised to take me hunting the next time he goes, even if . . . I am a girl."

Grandfather laughs as he says, "The ways of the Arctic have always been wondrous to me, but even more wondrous are the ways of small girls today. Welcome back home, my child," Ahloo continues, as he reaches out his hand and takes Kula's little, brown fingers inside his own, and they go inside the igloo for a good, hot supper of dovekie sausage and seal meat.

About the Author

Nancy Garfield Woodbridge authored the picture story books, *The Tuesday Elephant*, illustrated by Tom Feelings, published by T. Y. Crowell, and *The Dancing Monkey*, illustrated by Rocco Negri, published by G. P. Putnam and Sons.

She also directed several projects for Girl Scouts of the U.S.A.: *Worlds to Explore*, A Handbook for Brownie and Junior Girl Scouts, *Careers to Explore* and *From Dreams to Reality*, a Career Education Program, as well as *Juvenile Justice*.

On scholarship she received a BA in Literature from Bennington College in Vermont. She graduated with an MS in Education from Hofstra University in Hempstead, New York.

Ms. Garfield Woodbridge has been writing since she first held a pen at age eight when she wrote her first novel. She has recently published *A Bouquet of Fairy Tales*, *Hilary and the Secret Skulls*, *Poems In Exile*, *Stories from Around the World* and *More Stories from Around the World*. *The Islanders* and *Suns of Darkness* will be published in 2015.

Printed in the United States
By Bookmasters